THE
RIVER'S EDGE

THE
RIVER'S EDGE

MM ROMANTIC SUSPENSE

JORDAN CASTILLO PRICE

jcpbooks.com

Print edition published in the
United States in 2023 by JCP Books
www.jcpbooks.com

First Print Edition

ISBN-978-1-944779-37-5

1

God damn it all to hell. He dumped me.

Now, Carmine "Red Knuckles" Rossi wouldn't be the first guy to ever dump me, but he was the first one I hadn't been sharing a bed with. In retrospect, I should've seen it coming. Just like the type of guy who'd sneak out before dawn with my laptop and my credit cards, Carmine had made way too many promises.

"Stick with me, Gino, and you'll be a rich man."

"You're like the son I never had."

"You and me, Gino, we'll go far."

But promises are like kneecaps—made to be broken—so I wasn't exactly surprised. I cracked an eyelid and took a sidelong look at my current surroundings. Not only had Carmine dumped me, but he'd gone to some pretty great lengths to do it. I didn't recognize the stretch of the river where he'd left me to rot. Hell, I wasn't even sure which river it was. I tried to sit up and get my bearings, but my head spun, so I figured it was best to stay put. I'd taken a blow to the back of my skull, a nasty one. And even though an oily, rotten reek was wafting up from the murky water, the riverbank was probably the safest place for me. No sounds but the lapping of the water against the pilings.

I was alone.

Distantly, I recalled that you're never supposed to let someone with a concussion fall asleep because they might not wake up. That was what I had, a concussion. There'd been a *crunch*. Whatever it was that whacked me on the back of the head went *crunch*. A tire iron. Which wouldn't go *crunch*. But there was no way to know for sure it was a tire iron. Why I had that impression, no idea. But concussion or no concussion, I didn't have many options. Even thinking about sitting up made my guts heave. And so I closed my eyes and did my best to regroup.

The pain was sickening. But I drifted.

Some time had passed, I had that impression too, when I heard footsteps. Not the careful steps of someone trying to sneak up on me, either. More crunching, though not the type a tire iron would make on the back of your skull. The *crunch - CRUNCH - crunch crunch - crunch* of someone staggering around on the gravelly bank, all the while hysterically yammering, "Oh God. Oh God. Oh God."

Still flat on my back and moving as surreptitiously as possible, I patted myself down. The piece I usually wore on my right hip was gone. No big surprise there. Who would pass up a free gun, especially one with someone else's prints all over it? I'd need to improvise. Maybe the tire iron was still within reach. If not, push come to shove, I could always drown God Boy in the river.

Probably, it wouldn't come to that. God Boy's last "Oh God" was more of a croak, and the final crunch was different too, like he'd simply given up and flung his whole body down.

Maybe I wouldn't need my piece, or the tire iron, either. Maybe someone had already done the job for me and the other guy was already bleeding out. I gathered all my strength, shoved aside the throbbing in the back of my skull, and sat up.

"Oh GOD!"

So much for the bleeding out theory. God Boy wasn't wounded anywhere I could see. In fact, he wasn't in nearly as rough a shape as I was, given how quick he skittered back on his ass when he saw me move. But he wasn't much of a threat. Unarmed? Probably. Although his suit jacket could easily hide a .22, he wasn't reaching for a gun. Plus, he didn't look like the fighting type. He was an auburn-haired looker with a waifish build and a face that had never been shaped by the business end of a fist. Hell, he didn't even know how to hold himself, other than to grovel as I locked my knees so I could stand up and tower over him. "Don't move." My voice came out even grittier than usual. God Boy balled himself up to make an even smaller target. "You alone?"

He looked all around, spooked to high hell. "Yeah. I think... yeah."

"Who are you?"

"Shane?" He said it like a question.

"And who do you work for?"

"No one. I mean, I'm between…." He sighed. "I have an interview next Tuesday."

While I hadn't survived as long as I had by underestimating anyone, I suspected God Boy Shane posed about as much threat as a gun with an empty clip and nothing in the chamber. I kept right on posturing over him anyway. Old habits die hard, and I couldn't let anyone get the upper hand, especially with me still reeling from the tire iron. "You think I give a shit which Starbucks you froth milk at?"

"It wasn't a Starbucks—"

"Turn out your pockets, kid, nice and easy." I settled my hand on my hip as if the comforting weight of my Beretta was still there. "And don't try anything funny."

His hands shook hard as he patted down the front of his suit coat, attempting to turn out pockets that were sewn shut. If I had a conscience, I'd feel guilty for intimidating someone so helpless to such an extent, but my conscience was as long gone as my virginity. Shane's trembling hands fluttered lower, flitting over the front pockets of his pants, shaking too hard to work them open. "You want money?" he said. "I'll give you whatever I have."

I'd only been trying to make sure there weren't any weapons on him. I hadn't robbed anyone since I was too young to smoke—my talents fell more to the collection of outstanding debts—but I felt a telling absence of a wallet. My left back pocket was as empty as the holster on my right hip. "All right, stop stalling. Cough it up."

"I'm not st-st—" Shane hiccuped. His eyes went wide. Then he made a bubbling, horking sound, doubled over, and spewed out a frothing red geyser. This was not cherry Kool-Aid. Not tomato juice, either. I knew blood when I saw it, and what had just erupted from Shane was definitely blood.

White-faced, Shane looked down at the foamy red puddle, whispered, "Oh God," and keeled over.

Shit. The kid was in worse straits than I was. I don't have much use for cops, but if I got going and put some distance between us, I could call 911 and have someone see to Shane before whatever was ruptured inside him had a chance to bleed out. I knew it was just my dick thinking for me since, blood aside, this Shane kid was too pretty for his own damn good. Stupid of me. It wasn't like I'd ever have the chance to collect on the favor. But with a big knock on the head to use as an excuse for being such a sap, I reached for my phone.

It was gone. Like my gun. And my wallet.

Well, fuck.

Pain lanced through my head something fierce when I knelt down beside Shane, but I forced myself to ignore it. I was rolling him onto his side to keep him from choking when I saw what he'd puked up, other than the blood. From the center of the red muck glinted a single silver dollar. Now, it was possible the coin could've been lying there to begin with, and Shane just so happened to upchuck directly on it. But come on. Something had him all torn up inside. And what the hell did I know about the way bored and privileged Gen-Zers got their kicks these days?

I doubted payphones took silver dollars. I doubted I'd find a payphone way out here in the sticks, anyway. Still, waste not, want not. I pried the coin off the gravel, wiped it on a tuft of graying grass, and tucked it into my pocket. The absence of the coin left a perfect pale circle in the bloody gravel.

Shane didn't stir. I checked him over to see what else he was carrying. The back pocket on his pants was still tacked shut—either it was a new suit or he was a clothes horse who didn't want to ruin the line of the garment. But his front pockets were empty too. No phone. No wallet, either. Normally, I'd figure someone rolled him, but most people carry around odds and ends that no one would bother stealing. Change, tissues, sunglasses, gum. The pockets of Shane's brand new suit, the functioning ones, were completely empty.

Like mine.

I scanned the riverbank for familiar landmarks. There'd be some overpriced real estate nearby, wouldn't there? Everyone with too much cash was eager to blow it on waterfront property. Except this wasn't the sort of river where a weekend warrior would moor his jet ski. A dozen yards to my right, a tangle of overgrown weed trees obscured the bank, and to my left, a sharp bend hid the water from my line of sight. The opposite bank was lost in a soupy gray haze.

If there weren't any houses nearby, wherever we were, there'd at least be a road. Roads hugged rivers until they found a place to cross, even way out in the boonies. I was formulating a plan to flag down a passing driver for their phone and get Shane some help when I heard the distant sound of an engine.

I hadn't even noticed how freakishly quiet it was until the engine's whine cut the silence. I also hadn't considered how incriminating it would look if someone spotted me standing over some fancy kid who was sprawled in a pool of blood. But the engine sound wasn't coming from the road—or the direction where I presumed the road would be. It was coming from the river.

I needed a murder rap like I needed a hole in the head, so my first impulse was to duck into the trees and let the motorboat pass us by before some fisherman could make any presumptions. But I couldn't just let the kid drown in his own blood. Whoever was on that boat probably had a phone—or maybe they even knew the lay of the land well enough to get Shane to the nearest hospital.

Gravel crunched underfoot as I hurried to the riverbank. "Hey!" I yelled. The fog wreaked havoc with acoustics and ate up my voice, and the sound of the engine seemed like it was coming from everywhere at once. I looked left and right and started waving my arms around anyhow. "Hey! Stop! Someone's hurt!"

The small craft came around the bend, emerging from the mists, yet somehow the fog clung to it so I couldn't get a good enough look at exactly how far away it was. A hundred yards? If that. Close enough to hear me, anyhow. "Stop!" I hollered. "Damn it, stop!"

It was an open skiff, so the guy at the rudder should have

heard me, unless the outboard motor was louder than I thought. I jumped around like a lunatic and screamed myself hoarse, but the boat trolled right on by. Head throbbing, I jogged along the bank and paced the boat, straining desperately to wave it down. And just as the vegetation growing along the shore stopped me from running any farther, the guy in the boat turned, and he looked.

At least I think he did. But how could I tell, since he was mostly a backlit shadow, and he'd hardly moved? I dunno, but somehow I knew. His head had swiveled, and only his head. And he'd seen me. I knew that, too.

Behind me, Shane was now making stirring noises against the rocky ground. I forgot about the boat and turned my attention to him. His eyes opened. He squinted and tried to sit up. "Maybe you should take it easy," I said. He ignored my advice and pushed himself up onto his elbows. I shrugged. "Fine, suit yourself."

"Why do you care? You're robbing me."

"Unless you got a phone stashed somewhere clever, then no. You got nothing I want."

"Story of my life." His voice wobbled. One limb at a time, he got to his knees. He looked down at the blood, puzzled, then shook his head and scrubbed at his face. "Where am I?"

"Up shit's creek, apparently." Which I didn't find particularly amusing, since I was right there with him. I took a few steps away from the riverbank, cocking my head to see if I could catch any traffic noises. Other than the receding whine of the outboard motor—nothing. "Look, wherever it is we got ourselves dumped, the only thing to do is find a way out of here. Can you walk, or you want me to go on ahead?"

"No—wait. I can walk."

I wasn't sure I believed him, but it's a free country. If he wanted to try to walk, it was up to him. With my head pounding as bad as it was, I wouldn't be moving any too fast myself. And another pair of eyes never hurt.

Carefully, Shane stood and brushed himself off. He still looked pale, and kind of shaky, too. But if he did collapse again, at least he'd be closer to the road. "So what do I call you?" he said. "Since we've apparently got some ways to go—and since you know my name and all—it's only fair. Feel free to give me an alias, of course, if robbery is still on the table—"

"Gino," I said curtly.

His eyes fixed on my mouth as I spoke. "Gino," he echoed, just a breath. And I pointedly did not think about how something fluttered in my belly as he said it.

We trudged. The sound of our footsteps was way too loud, the gravel powdery and dry. I couldn't complain about Shane making noise, either, because my own footfalls were even louder than his—heavy, plodding crunches, no matter how lightly I tried to step. We'd walked for a quarter mile, maybe a half, when the piercing ache in my head forced me to take a breather. "Hold on," I said, and Shane stopped. He stood with his arms clasped tightly around himself, peering into the fog-shrouded trees. "Hear any cars?"

We shut our traps, and we listened.

Nothing.

Once the sickening pain in my head dulled enough for me to walk again, I motioned for him to get going. "There's bound to be a road."

Shane waited for me to come abreast of him and fell into step beside me. "But what if there isn't? Do you have any idea where we are?"

"Do you?"

"I'm not big into the outdoors," Shane said. "Last I remember, I was at some guy's house. Didn't know him personally, but he was a friend of my friend's cousin, so, y'know. A bunch of us."

"Pretty big leap, from a party to a riverbank."

"I'll bet they think it's pretty funny, ditching me all the way out here in this scratchy suit." As gags went, it was a lousy one. "But what I can't figure out is how anyone could have been straight enough to drive. One minute I'm blissed out—well, okay, maybe a little nauseated—heading for the bathroom. Then things get hazy, and next thing I know, I'm here. I saw your feet sticking out from the trees and I figured maybe all of us decided to commune with nature while I was blacked out. Weirder things have happened. But then I got a better look at you and realized you weren't at the party."

"No kidding."

"I would have noticed."

"Hard to miss someone twice your size and twice your age."

"Hello—I'll be thirty next month. And you hardly qualify

for a senior discount."

Thirty? I slid him a sidelong look. Good genes.

"What about you?" Shane asked. "How'd you end up in the middle of nowhere?"

Unfortunately, I couldn't blame drugs for my current predicament. All I could point to was my own stupidity.

2

Love is the closest thing to heaven you can experience on earth, at least while you're in the thick of it. That's why so many people keep going back for more, even after they've been burned. I'd met my last heavenly body at an over-priced cafe over by the second-hand record store and the yoga studio that keeps changing management. Literally bumped into him while I was heading for the john and he was bussing his own table. Dirty dishes went flying, a plate, a cup, a water glass and a fork. Yet miraculously, the two of us lunged, each to our own right side, and caught everything breakable before impact. The only thing that hit the floor was a balled-up paper napkin.

"Talk about being in sync," he said. And then he took a better look at me and gave me the old once-over.

When it comes to hooking up, I'm not usually the one to start things. I don't need to. Some people don't know eye contact from bedroom eyes, but I've never mistaken polite interest for flirtation. The guy with the quick reflexes and nimble hands was looking at me like a starving dog eyeing a steak. Just for a split second. Because it's none too safe to cruise someone who looks like they'll kick your ass from here to next Wednesday if they aren't flattered by your attentions.

But I responded the way I normally did when the situation permitted—sustained eye contact, a slow smile—and before I knew it, Gabriel of the fast hands and faster smile was figuring into my weekend plans. I'd pegged him to be about my age, but he was half a dozen years older, pushing fifty. He'd had a more forgiving life, one that involved a desk job, a gym membership and a skin care regimen. That might've rubbed me wrong, but in him, it didn't. He was confident, and he was sincere. And he was perfectly happy to let me be myself...the parts of myself I could actually be without putting him in the line of fire, anyway.

Unfortunately, he was smart, too. He knew something was up the first time I rendezvoused fifteen minutes late. In three seconds flat, warning flags rose from every piece of my story I'd neglected to share. Initially, he'd assumed I was married, sneaking off from my wife, my kids and my house in the suburbs for a little thrill on the side. He didn't accuse me of it directly, but I read it plain and simple in his eyes. And even as the idea occurred to him and he checked my left hand for the dent of a wedding band, I could see he realized he was wrong, at least about the specifics of what I wasn't telling him. He only knew something didn't add up.

Thanks, I told him, it's been fun.

That was that.

You gotta be careful when you deal with the smart ones,

and that's a shame. Most anyone can figure out what to do in bed. The clever ones are the ones who still hold your interest once the clothes go back on.

In the scheme of my entire life, I hadn't actually put in all that much time with Gabriel. A few hours spread over the course of a couple of months. But the impact someone has on you can't always be measured in the hours, minutes and seconds you've spent together. It was maybe a month after I dumped Gabriel and I was still thinking about him. The way his ass filled out a pair of jeans. The way his breath caught when he was ready to bust. The way the corners of his eyes crinkled when he smiled. But what I should've been thinking about in that fateful moment was Carmine Rossi.

It wasn't anything out of the ordinary for Carmine to have me tag along to a meeting and talk some sense into one of his debtors. He was well into his seventies, and his "Red Knuckle" days were long past. We'd made a handful of stops around the low-rent district, visiting shop owners for our various weekly tithes. We headed back to the Caddy, which was tucked out of the way, deep in the alley. Carmine popped the trunk and gestured for me to stash the cartons of cigarettes we'd been gifted by the corner bodega. Maybe five years ago, his hearing had started to go, so I thought nothing of it when he pointed past my shoulder at nothing and asked, "You hear that, Gino?"

I turned to squint into the alleyway and reassure him there was no one there, and then I heard it, all right. The crunch. Like the sound my feet were currently making as

I trudged over the gravel. Only once. But a million times louder. I mentally replayed the situation, wondering if there was any signal I failed to pick up on, any hint as to why Carmine would take his aggressions out on a member of his crew as faithful as me. Was I taking the fall for something pinned on me by one of those other lowlifes, or had word of my choice in companionship finally made its way around? Maybe I'd never know. And maybe I should just be grateful he'd taken the tire iron to my head rather than the .38 that had been lying there in the trunk right beside it.

Even if he did go to such elaborate lengths to dump me who-the-hell-knows-where. Probably to give me time to cool off as I found my way back.

"So where's the road?" Shane asked. Not like he was challenging me—but like he sincerely wondered. "We've been walking for…dang, I dunno. Seems like forever."

"We've been going uphill this whole time on rocky ground, and it's rolling under our feet like a bunch of ball bearings. Probably not covering as much distance as we think." I pinpointed a clump of gray, fog-shrouded trees and veered toward those. Our progress seemed more measurable with a goal in sight. We crunched along the pale gravel in silence, both of us determined to make those damn trees, and finally they were upon us. We pushed through.

Spread out before us was the river.

"All this walking," Shane said, "and we were going in a circle?"

"No. Couldn't be. It was uphill the whole time." Just a slight grade, but even so, I'd noticed it. "Rivers bend. That's all."

My experience with Carmine and the tire iron aside, I made it a policy never to turn my back and let someone lurk behind me. Shane had stopped walking, so I did, too. But he wasn't looking at me. He stuck to the trees, feet planted, arms crossed tight, scanning the river. He said, "This is the spot where I found you."

"It all looks the same. It's the fog." He was right, though. It did look a hell of a lot like the stretch of river where Carmine had dumped me, from the weedy growth to the pilings at the water's edge. I sidled a few steps closer to the shoreline, *crunch, crunch, crunch*, and a splash of red against the dusty, pale gravel came into view.

I know blood. There's plenty of ways for it to wind up in all the damnedest places. But there was something too familiar about the particular shape of this bloodstain. I tried to tell myself it was all in my head, but when I got close enough for a good look, I couldn't deny it. This was the blood Shane had puked up. How could I be so sure? The empty, pale circle, right in the middle, where I'd pried the silver dollar off the gravel. It stared up at me as if daring me to ignore what I saw, and what I knew.

Walking around for hours, and somehow, we'd landed right back where we started. I kicked the gravel, scattering it, obscuring the shape—pissed off at the river, the ground, the situation, but most of all, my own stupidity.

I should have known better. The phrase gnawed at me. Wouldn't leave me alone. I should have known better than to trust Carmine Rossi. I should have known better than to throw in my lot with him to begin with. I should have known better than to deck Robbie Milard for calling me a faggot in third grade, back before any of us even knew what it meant. And I should have known better than to relish the feel of that gap-toothed punk sprawled at my feet, blubbering how sorry he was. I should have known better. And look where it got me.

"Maybe there is no road," Shane murmured.

"We both landed here somehow, didn't we?" Sure, Carmine wanted to teach me a lesson, toss me somewhere out of the way. But he wouldn't be willing to offroad for more than a couple minutes. Think of the wear and tear on the Caddy. "We'll walk at an angle next time. And if we don't find anything in a few minutes, we'll double back. Start again. There's gotta be a road."

"Or maybe we should start building a hut," Shane suggested dryly. "That's what they do on reality shows, isn't it? Build a hut. Hunt for food. Scope out a source of fresh—" He gasped, backpedaled into the cover of the trees, pointed at the river, and whispered, "Did you hear that?"

Normally I'm hard to rattle, but at the sound of those words—same as the last question out of Carmine's mouth—my hackles went up and goosebumps rose on my goosebumps. Once I tuned out the thudding of my own heart in my ears, though, I knew exactly what sound had caught Shane's attention: the distant whine of an outboard motor.

The trees behind him would make for the best camouflage.

A few long, loud strides, and I took cover there beside him. As we crouched behind a thick screen of weedy growth, I wondered what the hell we were hiding from, and why the impulse had died in me to flag down a passing boat.

Gray against gray, the prow of a small boat emerged from the haze, angling toward shore. I'm no expert, and it's not as if I could recognize any distinguishing marks through the fog, but my gut told me it was the same damn boat as before. Maybe it was the general size and shape of it, the position of the guy at the rudder. Maybe it was the pitch of the engine. Maybe it was because, other than Shane and me, this boater was the only other living soul I'd seen.

Whatever the reason, I would've bet my last dollar (even though it was technically Shane's) that even coming from the same direction as before, it was the same boat, the same guy.

And whoever he was, I didn't trust him.

The two of us were so busy keeping our eyes on the boat, we didn't even notice the woman 'till she was practically in the river.

She crept up to the rotted pilings a couple dozen yards away, watching as the boat approached. She was older, Carmine's age, dressed like she was heading for her grand-daughter's wedding in a glitzy purple dress and a fat string of pearls. Shane and me, we were watching so hard we didn't so much as breathe. So how'd this old broad manage to sneak up on us—in her sensible two-inch heels, over a quarter mile of gravel? I would figure the whole thing for some screwy hallucination and chalk it up to the knock on the head, except that the way Shane's fingers were now digging into my forearm, I was pretty damn sure he saw it all, too.

By the time the fog released the boat enough for it to look like anything more than a hazy silhouette, the prow was kissing the jagged pilings. They spoke, the boater and the lady in purple, and though they had to be close enough for me to hear what they said, I couldn't. The woman rummaged around the front of her dress and came up with a folded bill she'd stashed in her bra. The guy stood—not rocking the boat in the slightest—took the money, then gave her a hand up. The boat had gone so still that it didn't so much as rock when she stepped aboard. She settled herself in the prow, chatting with the boatman, while he opened up the throttle and steered the small craft into the lazy current.

The outboard motor's whine receded quickly, eaten by the fog. I expected some kind of smartass comment from Shane to break the tension. Not only was I expecting it, I was hoping for it. Desperately. But when I turned to look at him, he was just staring into the fog, wide-eyed and pale.

I only realized he was still clinging to my arm when he released it, mumbling, "Sorry."

I half-shrugged.

"I hate water," he added. "Freaks me out."

"This stretch of the river wouldn't hold much appeal for anyone."

"True. It's the scariest dead zombie clown in the clown car. But I really, *really* hate water."

"Then we put it behind us and find the road."

I motioned for him to go ahead, then followed him out of the trees. He paused and squinted at the rotten pilings, and said, "But what if crossing the river is the only way out of here?"

"Then we walk till we find a bridge. Now, get going."

3

Straight away from the river, and uphill. In the distance, more fog. Trees. I set my sights on them and trudged. The pale, pebbly gravel crunched beneath the soles of my boots. Shane crunched along beside me. He was scanning the ground, trying to figure out where the old lady in purple had come from. I kept my eyes on the prize. Neither one of us had much luck. He spotted nothing but rocks. I misjudged the distance of the trees something awful. Either that, or my sense of time was all screwed up, because it felt like we were walking for ages, and the trees were still way the hell off in the distance.

"You know what's funny?" Shane said. The sound of his voice over the repetitive rasp of our feet against the gravel was a huge relief. "I used to think I was just born that way." I cut my eyes to him, wondering how we'd managed to land on *that* particular topic, and he laughed nervously and said, "Nervous around water, I mean. When I was fourteen, my new high school, St. Adjutor's, had this huge swimming pool. The gym teacher threatened to fail me if I didn't get my scrawny ass in the pool—Mr. Meyers, he was a big guy, all shoulders and arms, like you—and I flipped so bad that I totally cussed him out. I was so far gone I don't even know what I was saying. And kids, they embellish after the fact. I heard I called him everything from a drill sergeant that got off on torturing children to a limp-dicked Nazi on a power trip...."

We trudged. The gravel crunched. And after a good few minutes of that, Shane said, "Sorry."

"For what?"

"Babbling. I was just trying to lighten the mood."

We crunched along for a while, until finally I had to ask. "So why'd you stop talking?"

Shane paused. "You were listening?"

"Yeah, I was listening. Limp-dicked Nazi. He probably was. Gym teachers always spot the weak." Maybe I would've made a pretty good gym teacher, if I could handle the pathetic pay grade and snotty kids. "Then what happened?"

We continued on, trudging toward the trees. "I remember waiting at the principal's office for one of my parents to show up. Mostly, I remember wondering if I'd get in more trouble once either of them did. Not that my folks were big on punishment—they really weren't. Basically, all they wanted was for my sister and me to stay out of their way. Like we were the world's greatest inconvenience. My sister had this big, jagged scar across the back of her arm where she should have had stitches when she was a kid. Fell off her bike into a chain link fence and came home screaming her head off, gushing blood. Damn lucky she didn't die of tetanus. They didn't even take her to the doctor. Mom stuck her arm in the sink and told her to shut up, then went and watched the final round of Jeopardy with my father, who hadn't even bothered to come into the kitchen to see what was going on."

"Did either of them show up?"

"When?"

"At the principal's office."

"Yeah. My mom. She didn't seem mad—just annoyed. And when the principal was done lecturing her about the importance of physical activity and my lack of respect for authority, Mom suggested that it would be easiest to stop trying to force me into the water. Turns out, when I was a baby, my father decided to give me a swimming lesson by pitching me into a neighbor's pool. Said he saw it on TV, that babies figure out how to swim naturally."

Well, there you go. If it's on TV, it must be true.

"Principal never called in my parents again. For my sister, either, even though they caught her smoking in the bathroom more than enough times to suspend her. Funny. Back then, I thought all the grownups at school were just a bunch of assholes. Now I've gotta wonder. Maybe they were doing the best they could. Maybe some of them were even trying to watch out for me."

"Think so?" I scoffed. "Go ahead and tell yourself fairy tales if it helps you sleep at night. But you'll be a lot safer to remember that anyone who's in a position to fuck you over probably will."

"Suuure. Uh-huh. As if you totally ditched me on the

riverbank and let me fend for myself."

"Don't read into it. I just wanted another set of eyes."

Shane had obviously grown up with money. St. Ad's was a ritzy private school that cost more than my folks made in a year. That school wouldn't have thrown him out no matter what he'd said—they wanted his tuition. Whereas, in public school, kids' parents didn't get called in and lectured to guide their offspring toward the straight and narrow. If a serious enough rule was broken, the school would slap a kid with suspension. Expulsion. The occasional visit from the boys in blue.

Not that it ever came down to something like that for me. My old man had a fondness for "the belt," and I knew better than to set him off.

Always figured I'd learned that lesson well. Which pissed me off twice as much, wondering how in the hell I'd managed to earn a stiff whack on the head from Carmine Rossi. Once I found my way back to the city, I'd make it my business to find out. Lay low for a couple of days—enough for my head to stop ringing—then call in a few favors and see what was what.

Then again, why stop at that? If I was calling in favors, maybe I could arrange to find myself alone again with Rossi. Only, this time, I'd be the one with a tire iron in my hand.

I'd have to make it look like an accident. Decrepit old men like him, though...their bones are so brittle. One good fall and they practically shatter—

"Speaking of another set," Shane said with mock

breeziness, and my attention was jerked back to the present. "Do I spy with my little eye the same tree we hid behind when we watched that splendor in purple board the boat?"

"It's a tree. They all look the same." It came out nastier than I meant it to, because it damn well better not be the same goddamn tree.

But Shane didn't pay my tone any mind. "True, on the surface, one tree is a lot like another. Trunk. Branches. Leaves. But a particular tree that looks like a pig flying a kite when you cock your head just so...."

I lined myself up with Shane and looked right where he was looking, and....

Well, I'll be damned. It *was* a pig flying a kite. Or maybe a rhino. It wasn't until the kid tensed—and then went very still—that I realized I was standing practically on top of him. And that he'd made no move to get away. He would fit just right in the circle of my arms.

Which wouldn't do either of us a whole hell of a lot of good. He needed to be looked at by a doctor. Not pawed at by some dumb gorilla. I took a step back and grit rasped beneath my heel.

"Shh." Shane swung around with a finger to his lips, and I realized that whatever reaction I thought I'd picked up from him hadn't been about how close we were at all. He'd heard something. And now I heard it, too.

The distant whine of an outboard motor.

Shane eased behind a scraggly jut of weeds and I followed suit. He could've left more room for me...but he didn't seem to mind me rubbing up against him. There was no time to consider just how far he was willing to take it, though, this casual contact, when the sound of that damn engine was getting louder.

"I think I know what's going on," Shane whispered. "There's a loop somewhere. Has to be. Maybe something like, I dunno, a big island that splits the river in two. And this boat just keeps trawling around the island. Which is why it's always coming from the same side."

I could picture it. Made sense. Except for the part where we'd been walking for half the day. Out in the desert, or in the middle of a snowstorm, sure, I could see getting turned around. But we'd been heading in a particular direction. We had landmarks. So unless the river itself was nothing more than an impossible loop, with us just following it in a circle, this idea of his made no sense at all.

But it was more than I'd managed to come up with.

My head throbbed and the back of my neck prickled as the prow of the black skiff cut through the fog. It looked big. Or maybe like we were closer than I'd thought. Or...hell, I couldn't tell. Everything was so turned around.

"Listen." Shane clutched my arm again. Hard. "People."

And sure enough, I tried to pick out voices, and there they were, just under the drone of the outboard motor. A bunch of 'em.

Out in the mist, the boat slipped by, with the guy at the tiller still as a statue. There was no bob or slew like you'd expect from a watercraft. It moved like it was being towed along by a string.

I shuddered.

Once the boat had passed, Shane gave my arm a jostle and whispered, "Let's go see."

If there were people nearby, it stood to reason they'd gotten themselves to the river somehow. And if someone didn't offer us a ride, well...I wasn't about to take "no" for an answer.

We crunched along the riverbank, less careful of the noise now as the babble of distant voices grew louder. The fog was thicker than my old man's belt, but eventually we muddled through close enough to see what was going on. The black boat was tied on a mooring with a handful of people sitting inside, and another dozen forming a loose line on the shore. They were all different. Black, white, brown. Old, young. Up-and-coming, or down on their luck. The only thing they had in common was that their clothes were all torn and singed.

"What's with those getups?" I wondered.

Shane squinted through the drifting fog. "Maybe they're all extras in some kind of movie."

I might have bought it...if someone had been filming them. But no one was. Not even on their iPhone. In fact, there was no bus, no carpool, no nothing that could've brought those people here all at once. Just a guy at the front of the line in a subway conductor's getup. And one by one, as the singed, torn people ponied up to the black boat, the conductor would hand them each a ticket...which they'd hand off to the boatman not a second later.

"How are they all fitting on that boat?" Shane asked—not

like he expected me to enlighten him. Because the only logical answer was, *They can't.*

But obviously, somehow, they damn well could—and as they piled in, the boat didn't so much as dip. Its prow was lost to the fog, so I couldn't see exactly how the passengers all crammed themselves on. Soon, though, the last person had hopped in—the conductor—and the boatman unhitched from the mooring, gave his outboard motor a crank, and coasted off into the haze.

The atmosphere went quiet, totally still, and eventually Shane said, "We could have just got in that line."

"But we didn't."

He sighed. "No. We didn't."

He sounded so sad—so lost—that it stirred up some deeply buried desire in me to make things right. "And why would we? We got no clue where we'd end up."

Shane's hand slipped from my arm, and as it did, I realized just how long it had been there. "We'd end up somewhere. Which is a lot more than I can say for the place we're in right now."

Things can always get worse. But before I could impart that hard-earned wisdom, I saw the boat had left something behind: a dark shape jutting out from the sandy silt at the river's edge. "Hold on—what's that?"

Shane squinted. "Is it...a bottle?"

Together, we crunched across the gravelly stretch between the weeds and the riverbank. It took us just as long as you'd expect to reach it, too, with none of that weird distortion.

When things seem too easy, it's usually a trap. But before I could warn Shane to cool his jets, he was on his knees in the mud.

But when he pried it out of the ground, I saw it wasn't some pipe bomb or molotov cocktail. Just a fancy cut glass bottle with a stopper on top. The type of thing you'd find at an old lady's estate sale.

"I know this is gonna sound crazy," Shane said, "but this belonged to my mother."

"Belonged—past tense?"

Shane huffed out a humorless laugh. "My sister—Heather—well, the two of us used to steal 'em from the china cabinet to play potions master. She always got to be Professor Snape. Cruets, that's what they're called. Oil and vinegar. For all those fancy dinner parties my family never had. Anyway, I think Heather was the one who filled it with Pepsi and mayonnaise, yelled *Explodicon,* and hurled it at the wall... though she always claimed it was me."

If I'd ever pulled a stunt like that as a kid, I wouldn't have been able to sit for a week.

"The other one went right in the trash. Mom said you can't have just one. It was useless." Shane's voice went soft. "Just like us."

Huh. Maybe Shane's folks weren't so different from mine after all.

He pulled at the stopper a few times, but his hand was slippery with mud. Third time was the charm, and the bottle opened with a dusty sigh that made us both flinch.

"I wouldn't touch that—" I said, but he was already tipping the contents out into his hand.

A whiff of vinegar, and a tightly rolled piece of paper.

"A message in a bottle?" Shane said. "Heather would've gotten a real kick out of this."

Would have. Also past tense.

I didn't ask. Whatever'd become of his sister was none of my business. Besides, the moment was past, and now he was frowning at the slip of paper as he scanned it.

He swallowed hard, met my eyes, and said, "It sounds just like her."

"Your sister?"

"No...my mom."

4

The slip of paper trembled in Shane's hand. He cleared his throat, cleared it again...and read.

"Make peace with it. That's what everyone says when they show up with their casseroles and their empty platitudes, only to wait five minutes, then take off back to their happy little families until the dust settles and they can pretend nothing ever happened. Your father's working late again, and here I am in this empty house, all alone. Wondering... what have I ever done to deserve this?"

"It's not from your mother," I said.

Shane blinked. "What?"

"It can't be. You said yourself, she threw out the other bottle. When you were *a kid*. So why would it wash up on this riverbank with a message from her, way out here in... wherever we are. That don't make a damn bit of sense."

Shane turned the dirt-crusted bottle around in his hands. "Maybe not. But, Gino...it really does sound like her. It's exactly the sort of thing she said when Heather—" He choked back a sob before the word *died* could get out, but I heard the shadow of it anyhow.

But he'd also said my name. And I felt shitty for liking the way it sounded coming from his mouth.

And then he said it again—but this time, with a lot more confusion. "Gino...." Shane held up the paper. "It's blank."

He handed it to me. Our fingers brushed. And the second the paper was in my grasp, it fucking disintegrated. Not to ash—to nothing.

"God *damn* it!" Shane hurled the salad bottle toward the river. It hit the water with a dull splash. The water wobbled. And then, like the paper, the bottle was gone. No ripples, no rings, no nothing. As if it had never been there at all.

"Listen," I said, "take it easy." I grabbed him by the shoulders—he let me—and I gave his upper arms a squeeze. Through the structure of his suit coat, he felt wiry and slim. "There was no message. Just something messing with your head."

"Oh, and now I'm delusional? Or gullible? Or—?"

"Don't put words in my mouth."

"No one believes me. No one *ever* believes me."

"That's not the point—something ain't right here and we both know it."

"I know what I saw." Shane pulled out of my grasp. "But I can't imagine why I thought you'd give me the benefit of the doubt. So we just watched a big group of people climb into a boat that should only be able to seat six, tops. So what? Surely I'm incapable of recognizing a letter from my own mother—"

I'd never had much of a temper. Couldn't afford to. Going

off half-cocked because you took offense was a sure way to get yourself in hot water. There's enough ways to get in trouble without inviting more by being pissy. But Shane was young for his age—almost thirty—and calling him a liar really set him off. Whether that was what I'd actually said or not. "Look, kid, if you just cool down a sec—"

I reached for his arm and he jerked away. "Stop patronizing me—I'm not a kid. You don't believe me? Fine. I was getting sick of you slowing me down, anyhow." With that, he turned on his heel and strode off down the riverbank.

You can't force someone to use their common sense, and so I let him walk. Gravel crunched underfoot for the span of a dozen or so steps, then the footsteps died away. Because he'd stopped? Or because the hazy river swallowed the sound, just like it had the bottle?

I wanted to go after him so bad it felt like a fist had closed around my heart and given it a sickening squeeze. But running after him would only make it worse. His mind was made up. Once he cooled off, if he wanted to turn around and come back, he would. If not, no amount of I'm-sorrys would change his mind.

In other words, people do what they're gonna do. Expecting anything different would only leave you disappointed.

Take my ma, for example.

Somehow managed to "fall down the stairs" every time the old man knocked her up. But once, it didn't take. And along came me.

Things settled down after that. Probably because she'd

bought herself some time by having a son. But before long, he went back to his old ways. Ma tried to make a game out of living with him—*let's see how quiet we can be*—as we crept around the apartment while he brooded in front of the TV with his Schlitz. But now the old man had two easy targets to smack around.

Long-suffering candidate for sainthood, Ma was. So everyone said. But she could've picked up and left. It's not like we were living in the 1950s. Half the kids I knew had step parents, or half-siblings, or single moms. I pondered it now and then, whenever I spotted a woman in dark sunglasses big enough to hide a good shiner. And eventually I realized Ma would never leave.

Especially after I tried to slip her an envelope full of cash, enough for first and last month's rent and week's worth of groceries, at least—and she threw it back in my face.

You can't help someone who won't help themselves. Try all you might—people do what they're gonna do. End of story.

And whatever Ma got? She deserved it.

The memory of the look in her hard little eyes as she called me a good-for-nothing hoodlum was enough to make my head split. I parked my ass on a fallen log and stared out into the mist, wishing the mental image of her I'd just conjured could sink down into the river, like the salad bottle had, and disappear for good.

I was still wishing when I heard the gravelly sound of distant footsteps.

Shane.

He came back.

I was on my feet in no time, stupidly relieved...until I realized I couldn't exactly tell where the footsteps were coming from. Noises carried funny as they bounced off the fog, and at first, I got away with telling myself it was Shane—it had to be, 'cause no one else was there but him and me and the creepy fucker in the boat. And no way would that asshole hop overboard and come trudging up the bank.

At least, I sure as hell hoped not.

My hand went to my holster—still empty—and then to a fallen tree branch as thick around as my wrist. With a good stomp, I snapped off a length about as big as a baseball bat, hefted it a few times, and gave it a swing. Not one of the better weapons I'd ever had at my disposal. But it would do.

The footsteps got louder. Closer. And they sure as shit weren't coming from the direction Shane had gone.

We weren't alone—but somehow I'd let myself start carrying on as if we were. Stupid. One look at a pretty face, all cheekbones and stormy eyes, and suddenly I'm throwing caution out the window? You can't afford to be careless in my line of work. One bad call and you'll get yourself killed.

But it wasn't me I was worried about. It was Shane. I'd let him traipse off into the fog, *alone*, without so much as a halfhearted attempt to make him see reason. If anything happened to him, so help me....

The footsteps in the mist ground to a halt. "Gino?"

The fog shifted...and there he was. Shane.

Coming from the opposite direction.

I would've taken it for some kind of trick, if not for the look of utter confusion on his face. "But...how did you get ahead of me?"

"I didn't. I been here the whole time."

"No." Shane took a step back. "That can't be. I was following the bank, walking in a straight line." He wrapped his arms around himself, looking young, and scared, and way too vulnerable. He looked like he might bolt. And I'd be damned if I let him strike off on his own again without a fight.

The branch fell from my numb grasp and hit the gravel with a dry crunch, and before he could think better of it and take off, he was in my arms, slender and perfect and real. I buried my face in his reddish brown hair—his shampoo smelled like carnations—and said, "Whatever the hell is happening, I got no idea. But from here on out, you and me...we face it together."

Shane was trembling, and I kicked myself for ever letting him walk off like that to begin with. I cupped the back of his head and stroked his hair, and said, "I got you. It's okay."

"It isn't," he said reflexively, though he melted against me as he said it. "Not one thing about this is okay. But whatever you do, don't let go."

I'm not sure how long we stood like that, clinging together. But eventually he eased back just enough to look into my eyes. "This must be a dream," he said—not like he really believed it, either, but was hoping I'd agree with him anyhow.

"It's as good an explanation as any."

Shane's hands were around my waist. He wriggled one hand up between us and skimmed his thumb along my jaw-line. "If it's true, though—and I am dreaming—then there's nothing to stop me from kissing you."

Bad idea. He was only into me because he was scared, and I was familiar, and he thought I could protect him. And if we let our dicks lead us around, it left us vulnerable to god-knows-what.

And I didn't care.

Shane kissed with the desperation of a man with nothing left to lose. He crushed his mouth to mine and found my tongue with his, and a broken, needy sound escaped him as my stubble rasped against his smooth chin. I squeezed him against me hard enough to knock his breath into my lungs, which only made him grapple me harder. He threaded a hand through my hair...and then jerked back and shoved off me.

Yeah, I'd known it was a shitty idea.... But then I saw he hadn't reacted to a simple change of heart.

Shane's hand was dark with clotty blood. "You're hurt," he gasped.

Somehow, I'd managed to forget. Maybe he was right—maybe we *were* dreaming. But now that he mentioned it, my head throbbed like it was fixing to crack wide open. I back-pedaled, resisting the urge to prod at the wound myself. I'd already known it was bad. When that tire iron smacked me, I'd heard my head crunch. I didn't need to stick my finger in the damn thing and make it worse.

"Let me see," Shane said.

"Leave it," I snapped. "I'll survive."

5

If anything'll kill a mood, it's blood—at least for me. It might be an occupational hazard in my line of work, but I'm not one of those sickos who gets off on it.

Plus, I could tell Shane didn't feel any better than I did. Probably bleeding on the inside. Shane was a talker, I'd figured out that much. His silence was setting me on edge.

"I'll get my head seen to," I told him. Yeah, real big of me, I know. But what more could I promise? "We'll find the road, and flag down a car."

Shane pressed his lips together and kept on trudging along with his eyes on the ground.

It only made me more determined to convince him that the plan was solid. "Most people wouldn't stop for me, but they'd stop for you. So we'll flag someone down, and we'll say we were both in an accident."

"What if there is no road?"

"Whaddaya mean? Of course there's a road. We got here somehow. Didn't we?"

"Did we, Gino?" Shane stopped walking, raised his head, and squinted off into the fog. "I'm not so sure."

What the hell was that supposed to mean?

"Come on," I said briskly. "I got a good feeling about this. You'll see. Any minute now, we're gonna find the road."

We'd been walking toward a scraggly stand of trees for ages—or maybe it just seemed that way with Shane being sulky, and me trying to hold on to the way he'd grazed my lower lip with his perfect teeth—when suddenly we were pushing through the undergrowth....

Only to find that fucking river spread out in front of us again.

As if he could sense the fact that I was about to blow my top, Shane put a steadying hand on my shoulder, met my eyes, and raised a finger to his lips for silence. I was trembling with the urge to hit something and keep on hitting, but I focused on him instead—*his perfect mouth, his pretty eyes, and damn it, I was falling for him something fierce*—and I kept my cool.

With only his eyes, Shane directed my attention to our right. Moving slow so as not to give ourselves away, we eased past the tree line. The ground here was covered in a gray-green moss that was a relief from that persistent crunching sound. But someone else beyond the trees wasn't quite so lucky.

The crunch-crunch-crunch of someone plodding toward the river came on hard and fast. By the time we cleared the trees, we saw him. A lean, trim guy in a skintight wetsuit and sport sandals. He was tan—really tan—and his damp hair was streaked by the sun. Mirrored shades hid his eyes, and a tether attached to his ankle dragged along behind him. There was no surfing within a day's ride, so I couldn't imagine where he'd come from—still wet, no less...so maybe I was the one far from home.

Carmine Rossi must've gone to more trouble to dump me than I originally thought.

Surfer Boy crunched up to the pilings on the riverbank. They looked awfully familiar, I thought—but I told myself all pilings look pretty much the same.

I was still selling myself that bill of goods when the whine of an outboard motor cut through the fog. Coming from the same direction it always did.

Surfer Boy crossed his arms expectantly as the black boat came into view. The boatman was a vague black shape at the tiller, like his face was in shadow...but with nothing there to cast it. As the boat eased up to the piling, I could make out more detail. The peeling paint on the hull. The coils of gray rope in the prow. Hell, I could see right down to the rusty rivets holding it all together.

But I couldn't see the boatman's face.

Shane's hand slipped into mine, weaving our fingers together. I squeezed it tight. And together, we watched.

The boatman tossed a coil of rope toward the shore. It was a careless toss, but with an eerie slither, it looped around the piling. Hand over hand, he pulled his craft toward the bank. When the prow hit bottom, it gave off a hiss that made my skin crawl. But Surfer Boy didn't seem to notice that everything about that damn boat, from the rope to the guy at the tiller, was just plain wrong. In fact, he wanted on.

The boatman...well, he didn't stand. More like he *uncoiled*. Once he was towering over the prow, he held out a hand toward Surfer Boy. Not to help him on, either.

No, he wanted something.

Surfer Boy seemed surprised. The fog played havoc with the sound, but bits and phrases of their conversation came through.

What are you talking about? Of course I don't—

—the most ridiculous thing I've ever—

—what difference does it—

—don't you know who I am?

What started as a conversation was devolving into an argument. Or maybe more of a tantrum, given that the boatman just stood there with his hand out, still as a statue, and didn't fight back. Meanwhile, Surfer Boy was ranting and raving and stomping his feet.

"He doesn't have the fare," Shane murmured.

I dropped his hand to chafe away goosebumps.

Surfer Boy, meanwhile, kept right on arguing. And the last thing he said came through loud and clear.

Y'know what? I don't need you or your fucking boat. Fuck. You.

"Oh my god," Shane said under his breath.

I said nothing at all. Just watched, stunned, as Surfer Boy launched himself into the murky gray river. It was a shallow dive, but powerful—the guy was all lean muscle—and it carried him a good distance out. He came down with a muted splash and was already swimming. A crawl stroke, even and practiced, arms and legs pumping smoothly.

The boatman's arm dropped to his side. I couldn't tell if he was watching. He must have been. But I couldn't make out his face to know for sure.

Surfer Boy kept on swimming.

My perspective shifted. Before, the river was just gray water on gray sky in gray fog, and I had no sense of how wide it might be. But now, the contrast of a black wetsuit brought it all into focus. Wider than I thought. Wider than it had any right to be. How far outside the city had Carmine dumped me?

Surfer boy swam with the precision of a machine. Arms, legs, head, breathe. Every motion in rhythm. Until that rhythm faltered, and he dropped below the surface.

The water trembled....

And then it *erupted.*

Blood and bone and shreds of wetsuit geysered up out of the river as if the swimmer had just triggered an underwater mine. A gazillion little pieces. They arced high, then pattered down into the water with a mess of wet plops—so many bits, it sounded like the world's wettest drum solo.

And through the whole thing, the boatman just stood there, stock still, and did nothing.

Once the water settled—way too quick for the violence of what just happened—he took his position at the rudder and started the outboard motor. The propeller whined to life, initially smooth, but with a few chunky stutters where it churned through whatever was left of Surfer Boy. The black boat coasted into the fog...and was gone.

For now.

Shane said, "No fare...no ride."

But I did have a fare—a single silver dollar. A fare that had obviously been meant for Shane. My voice was rougher than it needed to be when I claimed, "I wasn't about to climb in that damn boat, anyhow."

6

I've never seen the appeal of a boat. Carmine Rossi had a 60-foot catamaran he'd bought, basically to prove he had the dough. He'd never dream of using it to ditch a body—too easy to tie it back to him if the dead guy ever washed up at the water treatment plant. Why risk it when a 16-foot fiberglass skiff will do the job just as well?

As far as I was concerned, nothing good ever happened on the water...but I'd been willing to let Gabriel convince me otherwise. A couple weeks into our thing, I'd accepted his invitation to the yacht club because their prime rib was rare and their Bloody Marys were strong—and also because it was so far out of Rossi territory, there'd be no way anyone from the crew would spot us together.

I'd had no clue actual boating would be involved.

Imagine my shock when he led me not to the restaurant, but the docks, where a gleaming sailboat with the words *Prima Facie* lettered across the back was moored. "Don't tell me you've never been sailing," he teased—and somehow I managed to not flinch when he caught my hand and ran a thumb across my scarred knuckles. "You've totally got the hands for it."

Sailing is a lot harder than it looks. When you catch a breeze, you'd better be prepared to ride it out. But once I got used to being dragged around by forces beyond my control, I realized I was actually enjoying myself. It didn't hurt that Gabriel found plenty of reasons to fit himself up against me as he taught me to work the rigging.

It was no 60-foot catamaran. But the single cramped cabin was all we really needed.

Maybe now we'd manage to stumble across a boat, if we just walked far enough. And maybe it would be something more than a crappy little skiff. Maybe there'd be a cramped cabin....

My memories of that afternoon with Gabriel were starting to feel as hazy as the fog over the gray river. But the desire to go belowdecks with Shane was crystal clear.

As if my recent failed attempt at tussling with someone from the other side of the tracks had taught me nothing at all.

Well, it's not like I plan on marrying the kid. I just want to set the boat rocking. And given the way he'd sighed into my mouth back when we were locking lips, I'd wager he would be down for it. But not right this second...given the way he was staring at the spot on the river where Surfer Boy had gone through the grinder. There wasn't any splatterhouse gore to see, but there might've been an odd sheen to the water's calm surface where the guy'd gone under.

"C'mon," I said. It sounded forced, way too chipper. "Let's get out of here."

"Why bother? We've tried following the river—both ways—and we've tried walking away from it altogether. But we always end up right back where we started."

"Then we need to try harder."

"Fine." Shane was just humoring me, but at least it would get us moving. He gestured vaguely at the gray landscape. "Lead the way."

Of course, it would be harmless to turn my back on the kid. He was about as dangerous as the Easter Bunny—but old habits die hard. I mirrored his gesture and said, "After you."

With an eye-roll, he shrugged and set off across the crunchy gravel. I fell into step beside him. We walked for some time before Shane finally broke the silence with, "Heather had an amazing sense of direction. Once, we were at this party, and things got a little too weird...."

Did he plan on elaborating? He was gazing off into the fog with a faraway look in his eyes. After a long while, he said, "I was tripping pretty hard, and she'd taken more hits than me. Even so, she got us back home. Eventually. Though the sun was up by then, and we saw people getting into their cars in their stuffy business casual, with their huge travel mugs of Starbucks, heading off for work."

"So you were close in age. Your sister and you." It was a calculated risk, talking about the girl like she was long gone. But apparently my hunch was right.

"Heather was a year younger, but that wasn't why I always

thought she'd outlive me. She was the smart one. Not, y'know...gullible, like me."

Whoever had made him feel that way...I wished I could reach back through time and teach them a lesson they'd never forget.

"She wasn't book smart," he clarified. "More like street smart. I was the one with all the grades—hah, you can see how far my perfect report cards got me. Anyway, Heather always had this way of knowing exactly when to bail so as not to get caught. And she knew exactly where to score, and where to steer clear. Only thing was, Heather never backed down from a challenge. Dumb challenges, I mean—the dumber, the better. Like, how many Cheetos can you stuff in your nose? Or, bet you can't get that guy to give you his underwear.

"So, when Luke Branston's parents were out of town in the middle of January, and he dared her to hop in the swimming pool...."

Shane looked so small. So defeated. Should I put an arm around him...or did he want to feel his pain alone?

"She wasn't even high at the time," he said defensively. As if that somehow mattered. "And where was I? Studying for my SATs. Because I'd bombed them the first time, and God forbid, with all my *potential*, I end up at a junior college."

So, by my calculations, his sister would've been sixteen—seventeen, tops—when she took her last dare.

"Maybe if I'd been there...not that I'd have stood any chance of rescuing her myself, obviously. But if someone had called 911 just a minute or two sooner.... Funny, though, you know what really haunts me about the whole thing? The dress she was buried in. This stupid pink floral getup. Heather wouldn't have been caught dead in the thing—pardon the obvious pun. Everything in her closet was black. But there she was, laid out in this ridiculous flowered monstrosity of a dress, all stiff and full of creases, right off the store hanger. She even had one of those pointy plastic tag holders poking out from the shoulder. And there I was, listening to everyone tell my parents how good she looked...and wondering if anyone even knew my sister at all."

We plodded through the gravel for what seemed like hours—probably just a few awkward minutes—and finally, I said, "Did you ever get to college, then?"

Shane shot me a humorless grin. "What do *you* think?"

7

We walked away from the river. Since aiming for something had only brought us right back to square one, we just put one foot in front of the other. Shane was quiet, and I found myself missing his chatter.

When he finally did pipe up, though, he surprised me by saying, "Tell me something."

"Okay...what?"

"What's the last thing you remember? The very last thing?"

You hear that, Gino?

Some things, people just don't need to know. "It wasn't as exciting as getting high at some rich fuck's party, I'll tell you that much."

"Exciting?" he scoffed. "No, that ship sailed ages ago. The first few times you jack up, the anticipation is half the fun. But eventually, it just feels more like...dread. Remembering that time you were well and truly blissed out and trying to recapture the feeling. And all the while, knowing you never will again, and you'll only wind up disappointed—even though it probably wasn't half as good as you're remembering anyhow. Chasing the proverbial dragon.... Oh, shit."

The fog shifted. And a stand of crooked trees came into view. With one that, from a certain angle, looked like a pig flying a kite. With some familiar gray pilings just beyond it.

Somehow, I couldn't find it in me to be surprised.

"Now what?" Shane asked. "When the boat comes 'round again, even if we did want to board it, I don't have the fare."

His coin weighed on me like a bullet lodged too close to the heart for a surgeon to cut out. "Fuck the fare. There's two of us and one of him."

"Oh my god. You want to *carjack* the boat?"

"You got a look at the creep on the tiller, same as me. He's not gonna do us any favors."

"No, I suppose he won't." Shane screwed up his face, then scrubbed at his eyes and sighed. "I just thought there'd be more time."

"Time to what?"

"If not to earn my way into heaven…at least avoid a trip down below."

"Now you're just talking stupid."

A dry laugh. "You're definitely not the first to say so."

"Listen to me." I grabbed Shane by the upper arms and made him meet my eyes. "You're coming down, and I took a knock on the head. We're just turned around, is all. And once we get our bearings, it's good riddance to that boat *and* the asshole steering it."

Shane patted me on the hip, then eased himself out of my grasp. "Whatever you need to tell yourself. But I, for one, know exactly where we—"

"Don't say it."

The kid smiled at me and I suddenly had a sense of how he might've been with his friends—pure. Not drug friends, but real friends. Or maybe his sister, if she'd never taken that stupid January swim.

And then he said, "Egypt."

I narrowed my eyes.

"We're in Egypt. Because yonder river," Shane gestured dramatically, "is obviously DeNile."

Before I could tell him to shut up and walk, something caught my eye from the mucky sand at the river's edge. A glint of light—some trick, when everything else was lost in a murky haze. "Hold on." I wrangled Shane out in front of me and walked him to the water.

As we approached, even though it was mostly buried, I immediately recognized the thing for what it was.

Another bottle.

Or, more precisely....

"Another...cruet?" Shane froze in his tracks, and despite my hand on his back urging him on, he wasn't about to budge. And the look in his eyes....

"What is it?" I asked him. "The matching bottle—the one that broke when you were a kid?"

He answered with a head-shake that was more like a couple of sudden jerks. "No. It's a different type of cruet." How many types *were* there? "This one's not for the dinner table—it's for Holy Communion."

I've never been much for church, but Ma was a big believer.

No idea why. Maybe because the priests claimed that heaven would make up for whatever suffering she endured—all while they were waving a collection plate under her nose. My old man had no use for 'em. Said they were a bunch of hypocrites. But he never forbade her from going—just in case God really did exist.

You never can tell who's gonna find religion. Take Carmine Rossi. Church every Sunday, rain or shine. And the priests not only absolve him of his sins, they practically kiss his ass over the big checks he writes to the parish.

Pains me to say it, but maybe my old man was onto something.

Guess Shane had more church in him than I did, what with the Catholic school and all, so he had to be curious what the latest bottle was all about. Which made the whole situation even more confusing when he turned on his heel and walked away.

"Shane—" I called after him, and he completely ignored me. "Shane!" He'd moved fast, with big strides, and my head gave a queasy throb as I jogged to catch up to him. "What, you're just gonna leave it there?"

He didn't slow down, not even a little. "I am."

"But what if it's important? It wouldn't just show up for no reason at all."

"I don't know about that. Random shit happens all the time. Houses burn down. People win the lottery. Why, just the other day, I poured myself a bowl of cereal and a petrified mouse fell out. If that's not random, what is?"

Not random at all, considering the drug dens he hung around. "What if it holds a way out?"

Shane glanced at me. "That's an interesting way of putting it...a way *out*. And not a way home."

Too smart for his own damn good. "Fine. No skin off my nose." Denial was more than big enough for both of us to get our feet wet.

Shane said, "It was probably just some random old piece of junk that washed up any...how."

We'd been walking fast, but only for five minutes or so. Nowhere near long enough to make a big loop. But there in front of us, beside a slimy black piling, sticking out from the silty gray muck of the shore, was the top of a fancy cruet.

Shane stopped so suddenly, I actually lurched ahead of him a few steps before I backpedaled to his side. His eyes were fixed on the bottle—and the look on his pale face was nothing short of haunted. Protection might be my line of business, but never because I cared one way or the other about Carmine Rossi. I'd just done what I had to do to keep my own skin intact. Shane, though—that stricken look— made me want to work someone over 'till my knuckles bled.

But with no one there to punch, the only thing for me to take out my aggression on was the cruet.

While Shane stared out blankly at the water, I reached down and yanked the bottle from the ground. The river-bank clung to it way harder than it should have, but I gave it a good, solid wrench. It broke free with a wet sucking sound, like the river had drawn a sickly breath.

The glass itself was cold. I wound up to pitch the bottle out into the fog and let the river take it—the same river that tore Surfer Boy to shreds. But Shane caught my arm and said, "Wait."

All my muscles quivered with the anticipation of hurling that thing as far out as it would fly. But, instead, I did like Shane asked, and I waited.

"I appreciate the gesture, Gino...but don't bother." Shane slid his hand down my arm and gently pried the cruet from my grasp. "No matter how we try to ditch the thing, I suspect it's just gonna turn back up again. Might as well get it over with and face the hymnal music."

He pulled out the cut glass stopper and a curl of smoke was released. I thought it was frost, at first, what with the cold bottle...but the smell of incense was impossible to mistake for anything else. It was the smell of Ash Wednesday, of a congregation dreading their return to dust, of a hasty black cross smudged across my forehead with the thumb of a senile priest, while Ma desperately prayed I would turn out different than I actually ended up.

Shane slipped a finger into the neck of the bottle and teased out a rolled up sheet of paper. His hands were trembling. The bottle slipped from his grasp and landed on the riverbank with a muted thump. He swayed as if he might pass out, and the paper rattled just a bit too loud as he turned it around and around, searching for the edge.

"Here." I pulled it from his unresisting grasp. "I got you."

Shane closed his eyes and nodded.

I unrolled the paper, and I read out loud.

"Dear Lord, I pray for the immortal soul of Shane Redmond and implore you to welcome him into your loving embrace. Shane was so bright—he had so much promise—but was always such a troubled boy."

"Father Dunn," Shane murmured. "I'd recognize his stilted, backhanded compliments anywhere."

And there was more. I read, "Try as I might to mentor and guide him, to give him the comfort and affection his parents withheld, his impure thoughts and promiscuous nature were always bound to get the better of him."

What in the hell kind of prayer was that supposed to be?

"In your divine mercy, please forgive any sins he may have committed—he had so many issues—and reunite him with his sister, his grandparents, and Your son, Jesus Christ. Amen."

Shane wrapped his arms around himself and stared out into the mist hanging over the water. He was quiet so long, I started to wonder if he'd even heard me. But eventually, he said, "For the record, Gino, I was twelve. I'd never even so much as jerked off, let alone been turned on by someone."

"What are you saying—this priest *did* things to you?"

"What else could I possibly mean?" He rolled his eyes. "I'd hardly be such a walking, talking cliché if I'd made it through my altar boy duties unscathed—"

"Stop it—stop it right now." Without thinking, I made a fist and crushed the note. When I flexed my fingers, it crumbled like a brittle communion wafer and disappeared before it hit the ground. I shook off the remaining scraps as I closed the distance between Shane and me and forced him into my arms. He was all stiffness and angles, with a humorless smirk on his face. He refused to meet my eyes.

"You know where that priest is now?" I demanded.

"Actually, no. A couple of years later, he was quietly moved to another congregation. Not by any efforts on my parents' part, mind you. I told my mother about what he'd been doing—and she decided I'd made it all up. For *attention*. Claimed the internet had given me stupid ideas, and moved my desktop into the family room so I couldn't so much as open the dictionary without someone watching me."

"There's ways of tracking people down." Some might say it's bad luck to rough up a priest...but I could practically feel the crunch of cartilage dislocating, the crack of breaking teeth, as I hit, and hit, and hit again, hard and fast, with no room for mercy. "He's gotta be somewhere close if he heard about your—" I caught myself before I said it.

But Shane heard the unspoken word loud and clear. So soft it was hardly a breath, he said, "About my what?"

I dropped my arms and looked away.

But Shane didn't take the opportunity to back off. He stayed exactly where he was, placing a single hand, palm-down, over my heart. "Even though Father Dunn will keep on getting away with it—they'll just keep covering things up and shuffling him to another parish—" He walked his fingers up my collarbone and stroked them along my jaw, coaxing me to look him right in his storm-colored eyes. "I can't tell you how touched I am that someone finally believes me."

He slid his hand around the nape of my neck to draw me into a kiss...and winced.

When he pulled back, his fingers came away sticky with clotted blood. But he was nowhere near as shocked by it as he'd been the first time it happened.

I said, "We'll get to the hospital—"

"There is no hospital, Gino, and we both know it. There's nothing but the black boat, the river...and you, and me."

As Shane spoke, he chafed off the blood, leaving a streak of rust red across the leg of his perfectly pressed gray suit pants. Then he took me by the shoulders, and dragged me into a fierce liplock that tasted more like desperation than want.

"This is a bad idea," I said, but it was already too late. Shane snaked a hand down the front of my pants, and my dick started doing my thinking *for* me. My breath caught as he worked my hard-on, confident and sure, maybe the only way I'd ever seen him assert himself.

He nipped at my lower lip while he jacked me off, breathing hard and ragged—nothing at all like Gabriel and his self-assured, easy charm. Nothing like the rough and random guys I'd get off with out back of the gin mill, either. Shane was pure need. And after everything he'd just told me—everything that had been *done* to him—I hated that his neediness turned me on.

Though it didn't stop me.

It couldn't. My own need came over me hard and fast in

response to the feel of his slender fingers gripping me just right, and the small, desperate sounds he was making against my mouth. Without missing a beat, I grabbed him up against me and hoisted him up, and he wrapped his legs around my hips like we'd planned the whole move together. I staggered toward the tree cluster without breaking our kiss. Whether or not I thought I'd actually make it, I had no idea. I just had to get away from that damn river.

We made it to the trees in a few reeling steps—the same trees that had taken us hours to reach before. I dumped Shane onto a tangled mat of gray weeds. It wasn't much, but it was better than the crunching gravel or the riverbank muck. He drew me down against him, me holding a pushup between his spread knees, him with his arms looped over my shoulders, arching up to rub against me.

"Touch me." Shane's voice was husky.

In the midst of all the wrongness, everything about him felt so damn right. Even so, I couldn't shake the thought I was putting my hands where some lecherous old man-of-the-cloth had already blazed a trail.

And he saw it in my eyes. His pale brow furrowed. "You think I'm broken."

"Don't be stupid," I said. When he tried to turn his head away, I took him by the jaw and made him look up at me. "I think you're perfect."

Shane's pupils flexed and his eyes darkened. "Then, for heaven's sake, Gino...don't make me beg."

It was the wrong thing at the wrong time—and most

definitely the wrong place—but how could I even think of saying no?

Our kiss was savage. Even violent. And just as I thought I'd taken it too far—that Shane was scrambling to pry himself out from under me—he surprised me by flipping us both over, straddling my thighs, and kissing me 'till I forgot how to breathe.

I grappled at him hard enough to bruise, groping his back, kneading his sweet ass. He slipped a hand between us to unhitch his belt, and as soon as the buckle was undone, I had his pants down. He was just as hard as I was, and when I made a fist around his shaft, he gave off a gasp that was nearly a sob.

"I need to see," he said against my mouth, then levered himself up on trembling arms. "Your big, rough hands…. Fuck, yeah." He watched, mesmerized, as I worked his cock. The flushed red tip appeared and disappeared inside the circle of my fist as I pumped it, and the slit glistened with arousal. "They're *nothing* like his hands."

It wasn't the first time those huge mitts of mine made me feel like a man. But never had it been for this reason.

"You too," Shane said. "I want you to get off, too. With me. Together."

I shoved down my pants and my cock jutted up off my belly like it was straining to touch him. I took it in my other hand, side by side with Shane's, and let him set the rhythm with his graceful hips. The act was as quick and dirty as any hookup behind a seedy bar with a stranger—but somehow it was so much more. Even through the clothes, I could sense Shane's wiry strength, and the way we would fit together, just right, naked and drowsy, tangled in sweaty sheets and watching the sun come up...if we ever got the chance. Which I highly doubted.

This hasty grope session would have to be enough.

Shane lowered his mouth to mine. "I'm close," he breathed against my lips, but I already knew, from the way his thighs had gone taut and the high flush on his cheeks. I jacked us both harder, faster, but it wasn't the pressure of my callused hand that finally brought me off...it was the look of innocent wonder on Shane's face as his eyelids fluttered shut and he found his release.

Afterward, I was worried he'd pull up his pants, make a smart remark, and start regretting what we'd done. But he didn't. Instead, he rolled off me just enough to settle into the crook of my arm, then nestled his head on my shoulder and breathed a sigh of contentment.

"I've given it some thought," he eventually said. "And I've realized this isn't Egypt, after all."

"Is that so?" I asked, playing along. Because Shane wouldn't be Shane if he wasn't making light of his own fucked-up situation.

I didn't realize he was actually serious...until he plucked a scrap of ugly pink flowered fabric from the weedy under-growth, twirled it between his thumb and forefinger, and said, "Obviously, we're in Limbo."

8

I might be a sorry excuse for a Catholic, but I did remember what the priests used to say about Limbo. Mainly because, even as a kid, I could never wrap my head around what kind of God would condemn the souls of unbaptized babies to wander around outside Heaven's gates, neither here nor there, for all eternity.

Shane and I were standing now. Him smoothing out his new suit with its sewn-shut pockets, me ignoring the bloody smear the back of my head left behind on the gray weeds. Both of us uncomfortable as all hell.

"Here's what I don't get," he said. "I've been baptized. I know that for a fact. Baptism, Communion, even Confirmation. My mother's got the photos she never looks at as proof that yes, indeed, I've dotted all my i's and crossed all my t's. Unless the priest who dripped water on my baby forehead was actually an impostor, so none of the other sacraments actually counted...."

He was being a wiseass while he said it—but then his face went just a bit too still. I could tell how he thought. Maybe not an impostor—but a priest with mortal sin on his soul?

No big stretch.

"If the problem was the priest," I told him, "this whole riverbank would be full of people clamoring to get on the boat."

"True. Unless...they eventually fade away."

"Don't go inviting trouble," I said. It would always find you soon enough.

As we talked, Shane had been toying with that scrap of pink flowered material, and he paused to consider it. "Besides, the same priest baptized Heather. I'd like to think this little souvenir means that she, at least, made it across. Though that would beg the question, why her and not me?"

Because he'd had the misfortune to cross paths with me before he met the boatman.

"I'm no model citizen," Shane went on, "but neither was my sister. We both lied. We both stole. We both did things for drugs that were better off forgotten. True, I had the opportunity to keep racking up sins a lot longer than Heather did. But I'd bet we both thought there'd be plenty of time to set things right before the final tally."

I slipped a hand into my pocket and fingered the hard edge of Shane's coin. Lying, stealing, tugging on some horny dealer's dick...maybe those weren't the sorts of things to keep you from crossing the river.

But sending a guy on a one-way trip to the riverbank? Something I'd done no less than four separate times?

Some things leave a stain on your soul that no amount of Hail Marys can erase.

"Cheer up, Gino," Shane said with a wry smile. "At least

we've got each other."

When I didn't have anything to say back to that, Shane chattered on to fill the silence. "I hope wherever Heather did end up, there's no devils and pitchforks. Not that I necessarily think the pearly gates exist, but some sort of classical afterlife, like Nirvana or the Elysian Fields? That might be pretty cool—not that I think she'd know what to do with herself in any kind of field, not unless it involved a bonfire and a keg. Or, how 'bout this? What if, on the other side of the river...the hospital we've been looking for actually does exist? What if the other side is a second chance?"

I made myself stop playing with the coin. Even so, it weighed heavy in my pocket.

"Kinda makes you wonder what that pissed-off guy in the wetsuit did to get stuck over here without a fare," Shane said. "What d'you think? Insider trading? Money laundering? I'll bet it's some kind of icky white-collar crime. He had that rich-guy vibe about him. In fact, I'll bet he drove a Beamer—electric, obviously, so he could feel all virtuous about it—"

As he spoke, a wind kicked up out of nowhere and the scrap of pink fabric flew out of his hand as if an invisible hand had yanked it from his grasp. We both grabbed at the air as it somersaulted away, and Shane was off like a gunshot before I could warn him not to go chasing after it.

Of course, I followed him.

Shane was quick. The heavy crunch of gravel rasped against my splitting headache as I lumbered along behind, and soon enough, his footfalls tuned to the squishy thud of the riverbank. As I drew up beside him, the scrap of fabric did a final loop-de-loop, light as air, then settled on the surface of the gray water just out of reach.

I grabbed Shane's fancy new suit by the back of the collar, just in case he had any bright ideas of splashing in after it. But with Surfer Boy's blowup fresh in our minds, I didn't need to tell him wading in would be suicide...so to speak.

The flowered pink scrap bobbed there on the surface, spinning gently....

Then all at once, it sank as if it had been sucked down to the center of the earth.

Through the wad of jacket in my fist, I felt Shane tremble.

Nothing happened on this river without a reason, so I pricked my ears for the whine of the outboard motor, figuring that asshole at the tiller was about to come coasting out of the fog and announce that Shane had a ticket out of this no-man's-land after all—and it'd been in my pocket all along. But there was no motor. No boat. No nothing. Just Shane and me and that murky gray river.

"C'mon. Let's go back to the trees." I gave his jacket a gentle tug and took a half-step back...and tripped over something sticking out of the mud.

A green glass bottle.

It was wedged sideways in the muck, but from what I could tell, it was smaller than either of the *cruets* we'd stumbled across. I let go of Shane, but kept my eye on him, figuring he'd have some attachment to it. So far, all the messages that had shown up—all the prayers—had been directed at him.

But Shane only looked puzzled. "I've never seen a bottle like that before."

Neither had I. "Maybe it belonged to Surfer Boy."

"Well, we can't just ignore it. What else is there to do around here for entertainment—with our clothes on, any-how?" He nudged the bottle with the toe of his muddy dress shoe. "You're the one who found it, Gino. You should do the honors this time."

At least it would put the question of insider trading vs. money laundering to rest. Besides, if we ignored the damn thing and walked away, I'd only end up tripping over it again.

I grabbed the neck of the bottle and pulled, half-expecting the riverbank muck to put up a fight, but the bottle slipped right out as if it was greased. It was a flat green bottle about the size of my hand, a drugstore aftershave with an alumi-num screw-top lid.

Relief churned in my guts. I must've been expecting some unwanted memento of my distant past to rear its ugly head. But aftershave had never once touched my old man's leath-ery cheeks, not that I ever knew of.

The screw top felt normal. Just a bit of grit where the riverbank muck had slipped into the thread. It wasn't until I'd pulled it off that the smell hit me—the medicinal herb smell that always clung to Carmine Rossi. And as I stood there staring at it like an idiot, a tightly curled slip of paper sprouted from the bottle's neck like a plant growing in a time-lapse video.

The bottle hit the soft ground with a stunted thud. But no

way was I about to let go of the message.

Because Rossi fucking owed me an explanation.

Bless me, Father, for I have sinned. It's been seven days since my last Confession. I've taken the Lord's name in vain—too many times to count—and I've coveted my neighbor's wife. But you've seen them low-cut dresses Rita Mancini wears. You'd have to be dead not to notice. And with Luciana going around dressing like my grandmother...well, who can blame me?

They were just words on paper. But with the smell of his aftershave stinging my nostrils, they sprang off the page in Rossi's creaky old voice, right down to the raspy smoker's wheeze that whistled through his turkey neck every time he took a breath.

The main thing on my mind—one of my crew had an unfortunate accident this week. No, don't worry, Father, you're safe. I won't name any names—and good luck to anyone who goes looking for him. Still, though, you think you can trust a guy, y'know? Then you hear he's been out meeting with a lawyer from Iceman Lysenko's crew every weekend and, well.... Don't loyalty mean nothing at all these days?

Lawyer? No clue what he was talking about.

"What kind of name is Iceman?" Shane asked. I hadn't even registered that he'd been reading over my shoulder. "Or can't you say, in the spirit of plausible deniability?"

Plausible deniability.

Gabriel used to talk like that. Fancy and precise.

Like a fucking *lawyer.*

And then there was the name of that sailboat of his....

I'd never asked about Gabriel's work—just some kind of desk job, I'd figured—and he'd never asked about mine. Had he known who I was—had he been *setting me up?*—or was our whole fling just the dead mouse in the box of cereal?

A shiver crept down the back of my neck. I chafed it away, and the skin was sticky with drying blood.

No, Padre, calm down, it was just the one guy. Lysenko's lawyer is long gone—probably got a one-way ticket to Russia. You seen them Russian women, all blonde, with tits out to there? He'll think he's died and gone to heaven.

Rossi didn't know Gabriel and me were screwing. He'd thought I was just blabbing all his secrets.

Never mind that the only thing I was privy to was who owed money and which kneecaps to bust.

Damn.

I'd had a hunch Gabriel would be the end of me, and I'd been right. Just not for the reason I'd thought.

And there I'd gone ahead and carried on with him anyway.

O My God, I am heartily sorry for having offended Thee,
and I detest all my sins, because of Thy just punishments....

The paper slipped from my numb fingers and fluttered down into the water. As it sank, the ink lifted off, swirling to the surface like the cigar smoke around the overhead lights in the back room of a strip club.

Shane let out a small gasp, and I realized I'd finally slipped up enough to let him get behind me. I hadn't needed to worry about the kid pulling a piece on me. Not only was there nowhere to hide one in that suit of his...but I couldn't exactly be done in twice.

He'd got himself an eyeful of what happened the last time I turned my back on someone. *You hear that, Gino?* There'd be blood, all right. And probably a lot worse.

Voice soft, Shane asked, "Which one are you, then? The crew member, or the lawyer?" Without waiting for an answer, he caught my hand and ran a thumb across my scarred knuckles as if he hadn't just literally got a glimpse of my thick skull. "I'm gonna go out on a limb and say it's the crew member. Which is good. 'Cause lawyers are the punchline of so many terrible jokes."

I cut my eyes to him. "And that don't bother you?"

Shane smiled—not the wry twist of his mouth I'd gotten to know, but a soft, melancholy thing that made my gut twist. "Whatever you've done, that was another time, another place...another life. Maybe, from our current side of the river, we can't reincarnate as some narcissistic social media influencer's pet mini-goat. But if we both decide that here and now, we're starting over...who's to stop us?"

The coin dragged at me like a cinderblock.

"Here's a thought," he said. "We'll come up with some new job titles for ourselves. I'll be Director of Strategic Mist Alignment. You can be Senior VP of Gravel Optimization. Just imagine all the perks—"

No doubt Shane's rambling would distract us well enough from what was really going on...if not for the whine of an outboard motor threading through the mist.

9

"Well, that's it, then." Shane patted down his sewn-shut pockets and gave a dry swallow. "Your ride is here."

I glanced at him sidelong. "*My* ride?"

"Leave no couch cushion unturned, that's my motto. If anyone knows how to scrounge up spare change, it's me. And it's obvious I'm as broke as the wetsuit-wearing douchecanoe that exploded in yon river. But, you?" He met my eyes. "You've had your hand in your pocket for a while now, and I doubt it's because you're up to something pervy."

As the black prow emerged from the fog, my gut clenched. I thought I'd have more time. Not to make up for the things I'd done...but to spend with Shane.

"The not knowing," he said. "The reason I'm stuck on this side of the river, I mean. That's the worst part. If I ask super nice, do you think the boatman will tell me why?"

I wouldn't count on it.

Especially since the one who was supposed to be left behind was me.

The dark boat slid from the fog with a waterlogged sigh. Up close, the prow was in worse shape than I'd thought. Its black paint was peeling away in strips, revealing a layer of worm-eaten wood that had no business staying afloat. But I was more worried about the boat's captain.

The thing at the tiller might be shaped like a man, but that was where the similarity ended. Looking at the boatman was like trying to peer through a window on a bright day. Maybe you could see inside. Or maybe you were just looking at a reflection. He had a face—I hadn't been sure he would—but the features kept shifting so I couldn't quite make them out. One moment he was Carmine Rossi (*You hear that, Gino?*) and the next he was my old man, hungover and nasty and looking to take out his frustration with his belt.

My vision shifted one more time, and then what I saw...was myself. Not a mirror image—but a thousand times worse. My own face, slack and bloated, staring up at the sky with filmy eyes

And I knew exactly why I'd had no fare for the boatman.

Good luck to anyone who goes looking for him.

Wherever Rossi had dumped me, he'd made damn sure I would never be found. That's what I had in common with Surfer Boy, whose body was probably fish food by now, and all his friends and family wondering if he'd just up and taken off to the Caymans with whatever cash he'd been embezzling.

But Shane, in his creased suit...Shane with the smell of carnations in his hair...Shane with his jaded sense of humor and the vulnerability he sucked at hiding...Shane got a proper burial.

He was supposed to move on.

He had a fare. How it had ended up in his belly, who's to say? He'd been embalmed, obviously, so there wouldn't have been any real blood for him to puke up. It didn't exist. Just like the broken cruet.

Just like us.

The boat idled up to the rotten pilings and a mooring line slithered out and looped itself around the mucky wood. The boatman didn't stand up, so much as flow into another position, like he was made out of the fog itself. I drew the coin out of my pocket. My hand shook.

Shane gave my shoulder a squeeze. "It's okay, Gino. You'll be okay—you're a survivor."

The boatman extended a hand—Carmine's liver-spotted hand, my old man's hard-knuckled hand, my own scarred hand—and I realized I had no intention of paying up. And also, I saw how easy it would be to hold that coin out over the water....

And just let go.

But a look at Shane's storm-colored eyes told me that if I went ahead and trapped Shane here with me, I'd never be able to live with myself.

Even if I was already dead.

"Promise me something," I told Shane.

"Of course—what is it?"

I took his refined, long-fingered hand in both of mine, and pressed the silver dollar into his palm. "Promise you won't forget me."

Shane looked down at the coin in his palm. "How could I possibly forget?" He casually flipped the coin into the air, and caught it neatly. "Ever since Heather died, everyone's treated me with kid gloves. But not you. Even after I told you about her, you didn't coddle me, or condescend, or treat me like some kind of needy victim. Or worse, they figure out how to use all my hangups to their own advantage. You were there for me when I—"

"Hold on, kid. Let's get one thing straight. I'm no saint. And you've got nothing at all to thank me for." I indicated the coin with a jut of my chin. "That fare was never mine. It's yours."

Shane met my eyes with that ironic half-smile of his. "I know."

And then, without dropping my gaze, he held the coin out over the gray river...and let it drop.

When it hit the surface, it didn't make a sound. Just sank into the murky water as if it had never existed at all.

That caught the boatman's attention. He looked at Shane with smoky features roiling through a series of faces too quick for me to see. I'd figured Shane would see the same thing I did: everyone who steered his life wrong—his dealer, then the limp-dicked Nazi gym teacher, then the priest—finally coming down to no one other than himself.

But maybe not, since Shane didn't seem bothered in the least. He held the boatman's gaze for a long moment, then smiled and said, "I'm staying here. With Gino." He quirked an eyebrow at me and added, "He obviously needs *someone* to watch his back."

Without a word, the boatman flowed into position at the tiller. He gave the engine's starter a tug, and the dentist-drill whine of the motor surrounded us. It pierced the thickening fog as the boat glided into the grayness, lingering for another moment once the craft was swallowed by the mists, until the sound, too, faded away. Shane wasn't watching after the boat, though. He was looking at me. And eventually, I had to admit, "If you think I'm worth sticking around for, you're sorely mistaken."

He gave an easy shrug. "But the important thing is, it's my mistake to make. Besides, since bottles are always washing up on shore, it stands to reason that someday we're bound to stumble on one that's got a few bucks inside."

Awfully optimistic of him to think so—but given the way his mood shifted when he'd locked eyes with the boatman, I had to wonder if maybe he was now privy to an inside tip.

Huh.

If that was the case, what if we weren't in Limbo after all— forever in-between—but something more like a trip to the big house? A stint with a beginning and, eventually, an end.

Bless me Father, for I have sinned....

Purgatory.

"C'mon, Gino." Shane held out his hand, and I took it in mine. "I spy a few trees in the distance—maybe trees we haven't seen before, or maybe the ones we're *intimately* familiar with. Care to place a bet? We'll need to use pebbles for our currency, at least for now, or maybe the honor system. Either way...let's find out what our future has in store."

I raised his hand to my lips and pressed a kiss to it. "All right, you're on."

And even though the gravel crunching beneath my feet was monotonous and grating, and the gray cluster of trees looked awfully familiar as we drew near, and my head felt like it was literally splitting—when I looked at Shane, and he looked back at me and smiled, I decided that maybe when Carmine Rossi dumped me....

He'd done me the biggest favor of my life.

ABOUT THIS STORY

I love watching scary TV shows and movies, but it seems that the majority of the scariness comes from the soundtrack. Seeing someone quietly walk up the stairs is not scary. Watching them do it while an off-tune violin skitters in the background is another story.

I got to thinking, how could I create that sort of creeping unease in a story, without the advantage of a soundtrack?

Sometimes I dream that I can't wake up. I struggle and struggle to open my eyes, but I'm overcome by this insurmountable lethargy. That's bad enough. But sometimes I do wake up...only to realize that, no, I'm actually still dreaming. In a particularly bad instance of one of these "can't wake up" dreams, after several cycles of waking up and then discovering I hadn't, I finally woke up, and turned on my bedroom light...only to realize that there should not have been a light switch in that spot, and I was *still* asleep.

That moment of realizing something apparently benign was actually really wrong...that was scary! Even without a soundtrack. So when Gino and Shane stumbled across the

same river, the same trees, the same pilings—those mo-
ments were inspired that darn light switch in my dream.

At least it was good for something. But the memory of
realizing it shouldn't be there still creeps me out.

ABOUT THE AUTHOR

Jordan Castillo Price has long been fascinated by Greek mythology. Particularly Hades, though she had a hard time wrapping her head around the reason Persephone was so gung-ho about getting away from him.

She has never found a message in a bottle.

jordancastilloprice.com